Tom and Francine
A Love Story

Sylvia Fraser

Illustrated by Eugenie Fernandes

KPk
Key Porter Kids

Canadian Cataloguing in Publication Data

Fraser, Sylvia
    Tom and Francine

ISBN 1-55013-944-4

I. Fernandes, Eugenie, 1943– .   II. Title.

PS8561.R36T65 1998   jC813'.54   C97-932059-3
PZ7.F72To 1998

The publisher gratefully acknowledges the support of the Canada Council for the Arts and the Ontario Arts Council for its publishing program.

Key Porter kids
is an imprint of
Key Porter Books Limited
70 The Esplanade
Toronto, Ontario
Canada M5E 1R2

THE CANADA COUNCIL | LE CONSEIL DES ARTS
FOR THE ARTS | DU CANADA
SINCE 1957 | DEPUIS 1957

Design: Jean Lightfoot Peters

Printed and bound in Italy

98 99 00 01 02 6 5 4 3 2 1

To Ming-Ting and Mika and Mika and Kobe,
To Pingers and Pong and Smoky and Oliver,
To Chop-Chop and Chou-Chou and
Chooky and Foo Foo,
To Miles and Mab and Magic and Hester,
To Barney and Gus-Gus and Guffy and Whitey,
And all *the other cats* I've known or never met.
—S.F.

For Charlotte T.
—E.F.

This is *the tale of a cat who is* rough,
A scruff-coated Tom, stout-hearted and gruff.
Born in a barnyard, with more than enough
Of what *the* right people call *the right* stuff.

This is the tale of a cat from the city,
A feline called Francine, snooty and pretty,
A maker of mischief, clever and witty,
But also possessed of a tongue without pity!

Tom hitched to the city by truck, bike, and bark.
He spotted Francine as she strolled through the park.
I've forgotten the time but it couldn't have been dark,
'Cause a frog on a bench was reading Plutarch.

Politely holding his tail in one paw,
Tom cleans his ear of the last piece of straw.
"Hullo, Miss, I'm new here. I'm looking for work.
I'm a pretty good mouser, fast and alert."

Francine curls her whiskers, decides she's offended,
Though clearly no insult was ever intended.
"You've got to be kidding. We've no rodents here.
The last one was put in a zoo just last year."

"I'll chase away crows so they don't eat your grain."

"What grain? We're civilized! Our birds are tame. Don't make me be rude. Just step aside, please. I don't talk to strangers in case they have fleas."

This is a pit bull who's nursing the hope
Of escaping his confines by chewing his rope.
He spies plush Francine with her tail in the sky.
His adrenaline surges, alarmingly high.

He bites through his cord, leaps over the fence,
Then sprints for Francine with a hunger intense.

Francine gives a screech—a real caterwaul!
She freezes, in terror, hump back to the wall.

Tom scoots up a tree to the roof of a house.
He jumps on that pit bull like he'd bag a mouse.
The dog takes off with a furious bellow,
Knocks over the cart of a wolf with a cello.

He zips through the legs of a clown wearing stilts,
Then ruins the wash of a goat hanging quilts.
He upends a hippo who's tying her shoe,
Then tumbles a haute chef into his stew.

A trolley bus crashes, twenty cruisers careen,
And a hundred police dogs converge at the scene.
They tackle that pit bull while he is still joggin',
Flip him over like a flapjack onto his noggin.

Now the chief shakes Tom's paw by way of citation.
"You've captured Spike Hooligan, scourge of the nation!
Our pups and our kittens weren't safe with him loose.
Why, he even stole warm eggs from poor Mother Goose."

Tom tries to return home the same way he's been
But this city's gone crazy, like nothing he's seen.
Cabs swish past, both sides, at a furious pace.
Tom's hungry and lonely; his fur's a disgrace.

But wait! Who's that calling to him through the traffic?
Francine, with her paw, making gestures emphatic.
"It's okay, my brave Tom. You'll soon be alright.
Just cross at the corner. It's safe with the light."

The cars brake their wheels with a deafening screech.
And Tom, tail upstanding, leaps into the breach.
He trots past that herd with its metallic roar,
And is greeted by Francine with kisses galore.

"You've taught me, Tom, what I've learned from no other:
It's not fair to judge any cat by his cover.
In this shallow world it is equally true
That it's wise to help chararacter shine its way through."

Since Tom needs a job, this next part is tricky,
For Francine must clean Tom of all that is icky.
Both ears, inside and out, and then that thick ruff,
Must be brushed to look manly instead of just tough.
With a lick on the nose that's purely affection,
She readies her Tom for her owner's inspection.

Francine finds her Mister soaking in his tub,
Working a crossword: "What's ten letters for scrub?"
Pouncing on the rim, Francine paws down his paper.
She grins like a Cheshire, with head wreathed in vapor.
"I've something to tell you that isn't so nice.
Your house, top to bottom, is filled with blue mice.

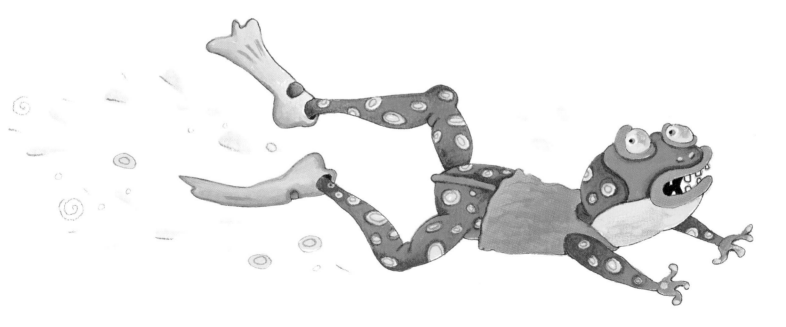

There's a couple in the kitchen, licking a cone,
And a big purple guy, boldly dialing your phone!
Two yellows are sparring in a drawer for one sock,
And a green-spotted bachelor has rented your clock!
Fortunately, I've a friend with a Mouser's Degree,
Experience, references, reasonable fee."

Since Francine is known to exaggerate,
Twist facts into pretzels, prefabricate,
Her Mister frowns while Tom looks away,
For though he can catch any mouse that is gray,
This technicolor species may be difficult to find
Since Tom is one hundred per cent colorblind!

The silence stretches, the room grows intense,
Till Francine can no longer stand the suspense.
With her paw to her heart, she falls to her knees.
"I confess, Sir, I love Tom, including his fleas!
He yanked my trembling body from the slathering jaw
Of a pit bull who wanted to swallow me raw!"

The Mister pats Francine. "You've caught my attention,
Which I suppose is the point of all your invention.
Tom's courageous and couth—no doubt about that.
We've a vacancy here for an honest guard cat.

We'll give him a flashlight, a hat and a badge.
He can furnish an office above the garage,
For I don't care the color or size of a mouse,
But I don't want a pit bull prowling my house!"

He picks up his pencil. "Ten letters for scrub?"
Tom clears his throat: "Sir, try rubadubdub!"
That's the end of this tale. Consider it done.
We've told you how *two* tails got to be *one*.